PERFECT FOR ME

HITEN BAREJA

To everyone, who believes that a person is
perfect with their flaws only.

Preface

No one is perfect. Everyone has their flaws. Loving someone is to accept that person with their flaws and that's what makes your love perfect.

Enjoy the book.

With Love,

Hiten Bareja

Acknowledgements

I extend my heartfelt gratitude to my Mom and Dad for their unconditional love and support. Special thanks to my sister for her encouragement. To my readers, your enthusiasm boosts up my passion for writing. Last but not the least, a big thanks to my best friend who always supported me in everything and kept me motivated throughout this journey.

CHAPTER ONE

A Train Ride

"When I met you for the first time, I thought you must have been very irritating and so annoying, but as our meetings increased and I got to know you, I realized that how stupid I was when I thought about you like that. The best thing I ever experienced in my life is your presence.", he said to her and then he came closer to her to kiss her.

She said in a loud voice, "A**hole, you d**k head.".

I woke up and yes, it all was a dream. My friends were trying to wake me up because it was my birthday that day. I woke up, looked at the clock and it was 8 in the morning. I told them, "Let me sleep, it's 8 o'clock.". But we all know how male friendships are. They brought a bucket filled with ice and poured it over me and said, "Are we morons who have come so far just to celebrate your birthday Vihan?".

I replied, "OK! OK! I am getting up. There's no need to emotional blackmail me.". I got up and took a bath and then me, Manish and Kabir went straight to metro station and while all this was happening, I was wondering about my dream and about my friends who didn't let me complete my dream. (Why does it always happen that when we are having a good dream, someone wakes us up? These people deserve hell.)

Before we go any further, let me introduce myself and my friends.

Manish- He is one of those people who always makes us laugh and is always at the forefront of bullshit but he is totally useless when it comes to talking to girls.

Kabir- He is the heartbroken boy of our group. Actually, a girl during our college days left him saying that I don't think it's working between us and we should break up....... Blah... blah... And our brother has still not been able to move on from that girl.

Vihan- It's me. A 26 year old man who's in search of his soulmate. I was a national badminton player in my childhood and now a successful trader by luck.

Back to our story. I, Manish and Kabir reached the metro station and we had planned to tour the whole of Delhi today. When we entered the train, it was completely full, there was no vacant seat. After 2-3 stations, the train became a little empty and then a girl boarded the train.

She was wearing a black kurta, light blue jeans and black sandals and she also had earrings in her ears. She was looking at her phone and I was looking at her. Suddenly a rough sound came from my behind which diverted my attention towards it. I turned back and I saw my friends fighting over an empty seat. I ignored it started looking at that girl again. She was looking at her phone and, in a few seconds, we reached our station which according to the moment should not have come. When I was getting down from the train, I saw her and coincidentally she also looked at me. We looked at each other and passed a slight smile to each other. Oh my god! How beautiful her dark brown eyes were.

After that me and my friends travelled to Delhi, visited many places and ate many tasty food items. While returning, I told them about that girl. Kabir said in sad voice, "Love is a lie buddy. I am telling you, trust me.". Me and Manish were very much annoyed listening to his heartbroken quotes from last 4 years.

"Oh, just shut up. At least for today please. It's Vihan's birthday.", Manish said. And after dropping them at their respective stations, I took another train to go back to my station. When I entered that train, I saw that same girl sitting there. At first, I was standing near her. When she noticed me, she asked me to sit next to her.

"I know you.", she said and I was completely shocked. Like how the fu*k she knows me. I replied confidentially, "So tell me something about me."

She said, "You are obsessed with my eyes, right?". Holy sh*t. How the hell she knows this?

"I mean yes. Your eyes are damn beautiful. I feel that they are like ocean because I am sinking in them since we had that eye contact in morning.", I said. Such a cheesy pickup line I used.

She laughed, "You're such a character." and after laughing she said, "By the way my name is Kaira."

"I am Vihan."

"So, how was your day?"

"It's my birthday today."

"Happy Birthday Vihan. I wish I was with you today.", she greeted me.

"Thank you Kaira and don't worry we'll celebrate my birthday some other day"

She gave me her phone and asked me to put my phone number in it and as I completed entering my phone number in it, she snatched her phone back and got off from the train saying , "Get ready." to me but why did she say so?

CHAPTER TWO

An Emergency

I reached home tired but the whole time I kept wondering why she said that. After taking bath at night, I slept and when I woke up, I saw about 10 messages and 5 missed calls on my phone which my uncle, Mr. Raj Chopra sent me. I opened his messages.

Uncle : Why are not picking up my phone Vihan?

Uncle : We've got an emergency here.

Uncle : Your father just got a heart attack.

(After 10 minutes)

Uncle : We are at Amravati hospital.

Uncle : Please come here as soon as you can.

After reading this, I quickly got up, got ready and left for Kanpur. I took a flight and reached Kanpur in about half an hour and I was extremely tensed. When I reached the hospital, I came to know that he had gone. After knowing this, I cried softly and started telling myself that I wish I had not slept and that I wish I had read my uncle's messages on time but by then it was too late.

My uncle and I completed all the rituals together after that. When I was returning home, I was thinking about my father that how much he loved me and how well he took care of me after my mother left. Yes, my mother died when I was 2 years old because she had cancer and she could not fight the cancer.

While I was thinking all this, a notification came on my phone but I ignored it. When I landed at the airport, I checked my phone. There was a message from a random number. I looked at its profile picture and it was Kaira's message.

Kaira : Hi! Kaira here.

Kaira : Can you meet me at Hazel's Café on Sunday at 12 PM?

(It was Monday today) I replied,

Vihan : Hey!

Vihan : I don't know what to say. I'll tell you by tomorrow evening.

At that time, all this was very confusing for me because my father had just died 15 days ago but I did not want to hurt her too. Next day I woke up in the morning, freshened up and started trading. I analyzed the data and brought and sold some stocks of a big MNC and made a profit of 10000. By then it was already dark. I made a coffee and started thinking that whether I should go with Kaira or not. I was very depressed at that time. In the end, I thought that if I didn't go, she would get hurt and if I went, my mood would also improve. So, I texted her,

Vihan : Hey! I'll come.

Vihan : See you at Hazel's Café.

She replied within a minute,

Kiara : Okay. I'll be there.

Kaira : Bye.

I woke up early on Sunday and got ready. I wore a white shirt, light blue jeans and white sneakers with black sunglasses. I feel very lazy in all this. I sat in my car and left for Hazel's Café. I reached there at 12.10 PM but Kaira had not reached there yet. So, I waited for her. I went inside the café and as I started walking towards an empty table, someone called me from behind.

"Hey Vihan.", there she was, wearing a red, off shoulder dress and she was looking so adorable, like I can't express it in words.

"Hi. You are looking beautiful.", I said.

"Thank you. You are also looking amazing."

"Have a seat.", I said and moved the chair backwards for her, so she could sit and then I also sat facing her.

"So why did you call me here?", I said.

"Can't I invite you to meet me?"

"No, No. You can."

"Actually, today I was free and I don't know anyone here so, I thought I would meet you as you are the only one I know here."

"OK OK."

"So, did you wait for my message for so many days or not?", she grinned said sarcastically.

"To be honest, no"

"Oh! Can I ask why?"

"My father died a few days ago. So, I didn't get time to think about it and I also thought that I would not come today but I didn't want to hurt you and I thought maybe meeting you might improve my mood also."

"Oh! I am sorry." And there was an awkward silence. So, in order to break it I asked her, "It's OK. So, tell me what do you do?"

"I just finished my college a few months ago and now I am working in a software company." And the conversation continued. After some chit-chat, I ordered two cold coffees. Then she asked me, "Won't you say anything about my eyes today?"

I looked into her eyes and replied, "No. Today I'll just look at them, until I see better eyes than them."

She blushed and said, "This means you will keep looking at them for the rest of your life?"

I smiled and said, "Maybe."

CHAPTER THREE

My Favourite Place

After chatting for a bit and finishing our coffee, we came out of the café. I wanted to spend more time with her. Meanwhile she asked me, "Are you free now?"

"Yes. I am. Why?", I replied. "I was thinking that today is my holiday and I don't want to get bored at home, so we both would spend more time.", she said. "OK. So, let me take you to my favourite spot.", I offered her my hand and said. She put her hand in my hand said, "Let's go!!!!"

We both sat in my car and I took her to my favourite place. That place was like a park, there were flowers in a bloom, there was a bench too, there was also a small lake and the sunset from there was also very nice but no one came there. It was a peaceful place. We both went and sat on that bench.

"Wow! What a beautiful place.", she said.

"Yes, it is."

She took some pictures of that spot and after that she asked me, "How did you find this place? That's damn beautiful."

"It's a long story."

"So, tell me."

"One day I was very sad because that day I lost Rs 1 lakh in my business. I was so sad that I just got in my car and drove out. I was driving very fast on an empty and quiet road and then I saw a child from a distance who was on the road. I applied brakes with all my force and my car passed by that child's side but my car got disbalanced and it crashed in a pillar and I became unconscious. When I opened my eyes, a woman was trying to wake me up. She picked me up to this place and started calling the ambulance. I saw that place and it was around 7 o'clock in the evening, I guess. I saw the sunset and It was beautiful just like you." She blushed. "And since then, it became my favourite place."

"Wow!"

"Can I ask you something?", I said.

"Yes."

"Why did you say 'Get ready' to me that day?"

"Oh that!", she laughed. "It's a long story."

"So, tell me."

"The day we met for the first time was my first day in Delhi and I didn't know anyone here but that day when I saw you in the metro, you were looking at me and it seemed as if you had fallen in love with me and then you left. I didn't think we would meet again but then when I was coming home after my first day of job, I saw you. You were standing right in front of me even though the seat beside me was vacant. So, being a nice girl, I asked you to sit beside me and that's how we met. And you probably don't know about me that I am very mischievous and I also have a lot of tantrums, and in a city like Delhi, I will go crazy alone. I mean who will listen to my blabbering? Who will tolerate my tantrums? Who will take care of me? And you were the only one who I know at that time and that's why I took your phone number and I said, 'Get ready' so that you must prepare yourself to be with me in near future."

"But why me? I mean, if you wanted, you could have talked to anyone else but why did you choose me?", I asked gently.

"I really don't know. When I see you again in the evening, I got a feeling which I can't express and because I saw you in the morning also, I jokingly said, 'I know you.' And then I enjoyed talking to you."

"And what if I disagree to be with you?" I said jokingly

"OK. No problem.", she said in a soft voice and fake smiled.

As soon as she said this, she got up and started leaving. I held her hand and said, "Hey! Don't worry. I promise you that I will not leave you until I found someone who has better eyes than you."

"Are you sure?", she smiled blushingly and asked me raising her eyebrows.

"Yes Kaira. I am sure." It was an unexpected promise that I made.

She sat back on the bench and placed her head on my shoulder and then we enjoyed sunset together.

CHAPTER FOUR

Bracelet

"What happened next?", Manish asked me.

"Nothing much. I dropped her off at her apartment and then I came back to my house.", I replied. Kabir and I were at Manish's house at that time. I told them all about the day I spent with Kaira and here is our conversation,

Kabir : Bro! It feels like heaven in the beginning, but later it feels worse than hell.

Manish : Oh man! Someone put a tape on his mouth please. And Vihan, do you think we are fools? You think that you will tell us anything and we'll believe it?"

Vihan : Bro it's not like that. Wait I'll show you her messages and her photograph.

I made them read mine and Kaira's chat.

Kabir : Vihan, this girl looks super cute. Leave yours and let me woo this girl.

Vihan : Nah bro she's mine.

Kabir : Can't you do this much for me?

Manish : Guys! Guys! Stop arguing over a girl. But I still can't believe that how, such a beautiful girl, gave you that much importance.

Vihan : I too don't know but it feels good to see her and meet her. A day before meeting her, I was very depressed but when I met her, I don't know where my sadness disappeared.

Kabir : So, what are you thinking next?

Manish : What to think about? Directly propose her, be a man.

Vihan : Nah Manish. I don't think it's the right time. I mean I don't even know her properly.

Manish : So, talk to her and know about her.

Vihan : But how?... Wait. Did I tell you that she left her bracelet in my car that day?

Manish : No.

Vihan : Let me text her.

I messaged Kaira,

Vihan : Hey!

Vihan : I messaged you to tell you that, that day you forgot your bracelet in my car.

I looked back and saw Kabir and Manish concentrating on my phone as if I was planning to rob a bank.

Vihan : What are you looking at like that? Am I preparing to rob a bank?

Kabir : Nah bro. I am looking at those beautiful eyes.

Manish : Those you are looking at, are not called eyes.

Kabir : Just shut up. Have some respect for your sister-in-law.

Vihan : Yours too, Kabir.

A notification popped up; it was Kaira's message.

Kaira : Hi.

Kaira : Sorry. I forgot my bracelet that day.

Vihan : Don't worry. It's safe with me.

Kaira : Thank god. I was looking for it everywhere for so long.

Vihan : Oh!

Vihan : Actually, I was thinking that, can we meet on Sunday? I'll give you your bracelet and I will also introduce you to my friends.

Kaira : Yes. I would love too.

Vihan : Okay. So 5 PM at my favourite spot?

Kaira : Okay. Well, now that's my favourite spot too.

Vihan : Oh! So that's our spot now.

Kaira : Can I ask something?

Vihan : Yes. Go on.

Kaira : Do you mind if I bring my friend along?

Vihan : No. It's absolutely fine. Me and my friends would love to meet her.

Kaira : Okay then. See you at 'our' favourite spot on Sunday at 5 PM.

Kaira : Bye.

Vihan : Bye.

I put my phone on the table and told my friends that we're going to meet her on Sunday. They got excited. I finished my work quickly on Sunday and started getting ready. I wore a grey hoodie, black jeans and white shoes. I picked up my friends and reached our destination till 5 PM. I saw Kaira and her friend sitting on the bench and looking at the lake. She was wearing a off white dress with a black blazer on top paired with black heels. I shouted, "Hey! Kaira."

She looked at me and came running towards me but her friend was still sitting there and looking at the lake. "Hi Vihan.", she said.

"Hey…. Meet my friends. He's Manish and he's Kabir." They shook hands with each other.

Kabir : Hey sweetheart. You are very beautiful and I must appreciate that.

Such a pervert friend I got.

Manish : H… H…. H…. Hi.

Why is he so afraid to talk to a girl? She's not a monster.

Kaira : Hi.

She gave me a strange look. I gave her the bracelet,

"Thank you so much Vihan."

I replied, "Welcome."

She said, "Come with me. Let me introduce you all to my friend."

"After you.", Kabir said.

When we reached there, Kaira said, "Hey meet my friend...."

We looked at her friend and said together, "Aisha!!!?!!?"

CHAPTER FIVE
Reunion

"What are you doing here Aisha?", Kabir asked. She saw him, got up from the bench, went to him, hugged her and started crying.

"Where were you for the last 4 years? I tried to look for you everywhere but couldn't find you anywhere.", she said. Kabir wiped her tears and said, "Hey Aisha! Listen to me. I am here with you, standing in front of you, so, let's go somewhere else and talk about it." He looked at me and said, "Vihan, give me your car keys. I'll bring it back in 10-15 minutes. I need to talk to Aisha." I gave him the keys and he left with Aisha.

"Can either of you tell me what's going on here?", Kaira asked.

I started telling her the whole story.

Cut to, 5 years back. We were in third year of our college. Our third year of college was about to start from the very next day. I was sitting in my room, preparing to go to college, when I got a notification on my phone. It was Kabir's message and a photograph was attached to it,

Kabir : Hey guys! Listen to me. Today I saw a very beautiful girl in our college. She is a new comer.

Kabir : (Aisha's photograph)

Kabir : Look at her. She is damn cute.

Manish : Then go talk too her, otherwise some other boy will woo her and then you will come to us with your sad shit that 'I should have talked to her earlier'.

Kabir : Nah Manish. What if I got rejected? My self esteem will be blown in pieces.

Vihan : Kabir, just relax. Leave it on me.

Kabir : Okay.

So being a good friend, next day I met Aisha in college. I told her everything that what Kabir feels about her. She said, "I don't want anything more than friendship right now. If he's willing to be my friend then it's OK."

"But why don't you want to come in a relationship?", I asked respectfully.

"Because I have just come to this college and I don't even know this guy properly."

"Oh! No problem. By the way, can I have your number, so that I can update you time-to-time.?"

"I hope this is not a trick to get my number."

"If you don't want to give your number, then it's okay. I don't have any problem.

"No-No. I was just kidding. Give me your phone."

She entered her phone number in my phone and we went our respective ways. I went to Kabir and told him everything. "It's OK. I think, she wants to know me before getting into a relationship.", he said.

"Okay. So, I am fixing your date with Aisha on Saturday after college.", I said. "And one more thing, treat her only like your friend, not like your girlfriend." I gave him some dating tips. I haven't been in a relationship yet but I still have a lot of knowledge regarding all these things. #LoveGuru

I texted her and fixed a date for them at The Magic Café and that's how they met for the first time. In a short period of time, we all became very good friends. Even Manish did not hesitate to talk to her. But looking at Kabir and Aisha, it seemed that they are not only-friends. They used to talk everyday for 4-5 hours and they also used to meet each other privately. One day we all were playing 'Face the truth' and this was the only chance, Manish and I had, to find out, whether Kabir and Aisha are in a relationship or not. Game begins and after some turns, I finally got a chance. I asked Aisha, "Are you guys in a relationship with each other?"

Aisha got surprised and said, "I am not going to answer that question. Ask me something else."

"Rules are rules, Aisha", Manish interrupted.

"Yes. We are in a relationship for about 3 months.", Aisha hesitatingly said.

"Why didn't you guys tell us?", I asked.

"Because we wanted to keep it private, Vihan. And because now you both know about our relationship, do not tell about this to anyone.", Kabir said.

Manish and I agreed with Kabir's statement and continued our game.

We all created so much memories in our college days. Some good, some bad. One day, Kabir came to my room and he was looking very depressed. Manish asked, "What happened? Did you again have a fight with Aisha?"

"No", he replied. "Then what happened?", Manish asked once again.

"Aisha said that it wasn't working between us and she wanted to break up with me."

"Wait! What?", I reacted.

"Yes, Vihan and from now onwards, no one will talk about Aisha. Can you guys leave me alone for some time?"

We got out of the room quietly without saying a word further. I messaged Aisha but she didn't reply back. Later I came to know that she left our college and she wasn't having her old mobile number. Since then, we guys haven't spoken a single word regarding Aisha in front of Kabir.

Back to the present day,

"Oh! That's so sad.", Kaira said.

"Yeah it is but we cannot do anything about it.", I replied. "And how do you know Aisha?"

"She's works in my office and when I met her, I came to know that she also lives in my apartment.", she replied.

Then suddenly I got a notification on my phone,

Kabir : Hey Vihan! Can you take a cab for today please? I'll come at your place along with your car tomorrow.

Vihan : But you said that, you will come back within 15 minutes.

Kabir : Please try to understand Vihan.

Vihan : Okay. Fine.

CHAPTER SIX

Planning

I reached my home by 9 PM and I was very much confused about what happened today. On the other hand, I was also tensed about my car. I had my dinner and slept. Next day, I got up and get ready for my work. While I was working, around 1 PM, I saw Kabir in my car from my window. He came inside my house and gave me my car keys without saying a word.

"What happened yesterday?", I asked. He replied, "Nothing much."

He was looking very different so I asked him once again, "You can tell me. I am here with you."

"I lied to you.", he said.

"What?"

"Yes. 3 years ago, when I told you that Aisha broke up with me, it was not true. Actually I broke up with her."

"But Why?"

"Day before our break up, she called me and asked me to meet her because she had to tell me something important. So we decided to meet the very next day. I went there and she told me that she was leaving this college because her parents want her to go to abroad for her further studies. She also told me that she tried very hard to convince her but she failed and I was very upset and angry at that time. I asked her to not go but she was all set to leave. She told me that we'll meet in every 6 months and video call each other everyday but I was not comfortable. We argued for about 20 minutes and then I said that Long distance relationships don't work and I don't want to be a part of this long distance thing. She tried to convince me but I was very angry at that time and that's why I decided to break up with her against my will and blocked her from everywhere."

"Oh! But what happened yesterday?"

"I took Aisha to a Café and there she told me that she had been looking for me, for the last one year. Then she told me that she still loves me and wants to marry me. I said that I'll think about it. We went for a drive and talked about our past. I dropped her at her apartment and she seemed very happy after meeting me."

"Are you happy?"

"I can't express it words but yes, I am happy."

"Oh! So what about marriage proposal?"

"I love her Vihan but...."

"There are no ifs and buts in love. You love her, she loves you and you will handle everything like our college days."

"Okay. I'll think about it."

He left and I started my work again. After completing my work, I made a coffee for myself. It was about 11.30 at that time and I was thinking about Kaira and I came up with an idea. I called Kaira and she was talking in a low voice.

Vihan : Hi.

Kaira : Hey.

Vihan : I have an idea.

Kaira : What idea?

I told her everything what Kabir told me.

Kaira : Oh! So what's the idea?

Vihan : I was thinking that we should plan a reunion party for them.

Kaira : That sounds great.

Vihan : And there, Kabir will propose her.

Kaira : Wow! It will be so romantic.

Vihan : Yes. So will you help me?

Kaira : Yes, I will.

Vihan : What happened? Are you fine?

Kaira : Nothing much Vihan.

Vihan : You can tell me Kaira.

Kaira : Actually I was very tensed about my tomorrow's meeting and it is really important for me.

Vihan : Don't worry. I have a solution.

Kaira : What solution?

Vihan : Would you like to listen some songs with me? I heard that listening songs with someone makes you relaxed.

Kaira : Okay. We'll play songs one by one. Let's start with you.

We listened to some songs. I was sitting in my balcony and looking at the moon. I asked her, "Do you sing?"

"Yes."

"Then sing a song for me."

"Are you mad Vihan?"

"No, I am desperate to hear a song from you."

"Okayyyyy"

She sang a romantic song for me and at the same time I was looking at the moon and listening to her melodious song.

"That was really awesome."

"Don't make me blush once again and thanks for your advice."

"No problem ma'am."
"Shut up, stupid.", she said and laughed.

CHAPTER SEVEN

Prince and Princess

"How was your meeting?", I asked Kaira. We decided to meet after her meeting. I picked her from her office to drop her at her apartment.

"It was fantastic. All credit goes to you and your advice.",She replied. "So when is the proposal party?"

"I was also thinking the same... Wait! Christmas is coming. How about that?"

"That's good. So what's the plan?"

"I have thought about it. I'll ask Kabir to pick Aisha from her apartment. In between they will have a conversation and I'll tell Kabir to make that conversation a bit romantic. When they will reach the given location, we all will be there except Manish. He'll come after they'll arrive. He'll come and give Aisha a paper on which a romantic paragraph will be written by Kabir, and when she'll read it and look at Kabir, he'll propose her. Is it okay?"

"Yes, it is."

Her apartment came and she got out of my car. She said, "Tell Kabir and Manish about the plan and I'll see you later."

"Okay, bye. Have a great day."

I was about to leave but suddenly she called me, "Vihan! Listen!"

I said, "Yes, what happened?"

"Actually my mom and dad are coming tomorrow and I told them about you. So they asked me to introduce you to them. Will you come tomorrow?"

"Yes, I would love to meet them."

"So tomorrow 8 PM for dinner? Will it be okay?"

"Yeah, sure"

"Okay see you tomorrow."

"Bye."

"Bye-bye."

I reached my home and called Kabir and Manish,

Vihan : Hey both of you, listen to me carefully.

Manish : Go on.

I told them about the plan.

Kabir : It's good.

Manish : I'll write that paragraph for her from Kabir's side.

Kabir : Absolutely not.

Manish : But why?

Kabir : I don't trust you in this thing. You will write something rubbish.

Vihan : Wait Manish. We'll let you write. First tell me, why do you want to write?

Manish : I want to improve my romantic skills. Hehehe.

Kabir : Okay you can write but if you wrote something rubbish, I swear I'll kill you.

Manish : You can trust me.

Vihan : Okay now listen Kabir. Firstly, are you ready for this marriage?

Kabir : Yes, I am.

Vihan : Okay. Secondly, I need a help from you Kabir.

Kabir : What happened?

Vihan : Actually, tomorrow I am going to meet Kaira's parents. So I need some tips from you because I am feeling very nervous.

Manish : You are also getting married?

Vihan : No No. They just want to meet me.

Kabir : Oh! That's easy. Treat them with respect and care and they'll be happy. Here's a tip. Take a bouquet of flowers for them.

Manish : Does Kaira have any sister?

Vihan : Shut up. You pervert.

Kabir : Don't worry. Just relax.

Vihan : Okay. Wish me luck.

Next day, I reached Kaira's apartment with a bouquet of red and white flowers. I wore a white shirt, black pants and black formal shoes. It was a formal look. I rang the door bell and her mother opened the door. I noticed that Kaira looks as same as her mother. Her mother looked at me and asked, "Are you Vihan?"

"Yes aunty. I am Vihan."

I took her blessings and gave her the bouquet. She asked me to come in. I entered inside and her father was sitting on a sofa watching a cricket match between India and Australia. He was so much focused that he don't even noticed me. Her mother told me to sit down. "Hey listen. He's Vihan.", Kaira's mother said to Kaira's father.

"Oh, here you are my son."

He greeted me with a handshake.

"Do you watch cricket?", He asked.

"Sometimes.", I replied.

Her mother brought a glass of water for me.

"By the way, Kaira told us a lot about you.", Her mother said.

"What did she told you aunty?"

"She told us that how you take care of her, spend time with her and you were her first friend in this city. She really likes you a lot.", Her mother said.

I said, "Thank you aunty."

Kaira came out of her room. She was wearing a black saree and damn, she was looking amazing. She looked at all of us and asked her father, "How am I looking dad?"

"Like a princess.", he replied.

"But I don't have my prince Dad."

"Don't worry Kaira. One day you will definitely get a prince like Vihan."

"Don't tease me Dad."

I was shocked by his reply but at the same time, Kaira looked at me, I looked at her and we both smiled and blushed.

CHAPTER EIGHT

Like or Love

"How's the food Vihan?", Kaira's mother asked. We all were on the dining table having dinner.

"It's amazing Aunty but the gulab jamun is a little too sweet.", I said.

"Oh, sorry about that. Actually Kaira likes sweets very much."

"No problem Aunty. I rarely eat sweets. By the way, I must say that your family is very friendly."

"Well it's our family philosophy. Treat those people well who talk to you politely with respect and maintain distance who don't.", Her father said.

"What do you do for living?", Her mother asked.

"Actually I am a trader."

"What does it mean?"

"I buy stocks and sell them."

"You are explaining this to someone who doesn't have a brain.", Her father said teasing her mother.

"Shut up."

"You are really a funny person uncle.", I said and grinned. I looked at Kaira. She was looking at her plate and smiling but then suddenly she stopped smiling and made a serious face.

We completed our dinner and I wanted to talk to Kaira. So I asked her father, "Uncle!"

"Yes son."

"Can I go for a walk with Kaira?"

"Yeah sure. Kaira will drop you at your car but only if she wants too."

Kaira made a shy face and said, "Okay. Let's go."

We were walking and walking and walking. She was smiling but not saying anything and I was also not saying anything. While I was thinking about this silence, she said, "So you don't like sweets?"

"I like but I eat them rarely."

"Oh!"

"By the way, someone likes me and didn't even told me."

"Come on. My mom told you this?"

"Yeah."

"Okay. I mean, yeah, I like you. You make me feel special and after my family, you are the only person I trust."

"So you don't love me? Right?"

"Is there any difference between them?"

"Yes."

"Elaborate please."

"When you like someone, you want that person in your life but if you love them, you want that person to be happy, whether they are in your life or not."

"Oh!"

"So you like me or love me?"

"I can't say."

"You can tell me."

"Why do you want to know? First tell me, do you love me or not?"

"I......"

A call came on her phone, "Actually I have to go Vihan, it's urgent."

"No problem."

"So, bye. We'll meet soon."

"Yeah, bye"

I went to my home and I was very curious about that phone call. Was he Kaira's boyfriend or someone else? No no he can't be Kaira's boyfriend. But suddenly I started overthinking.

I changed my clothes and made a coffee. After a few minutes of overthinking, I slept. I woke up and started working. Christmas was only a week far. I called Manish,

Vihan : Did you completed the speech?

Manish : Actually, I am in my office. I have completed it almost.

Vihan : Okay. Bye.

I texted everyone to meet at a given location at 5 PM on Christmas. I pinned the location. I tried to call Kaira but she didn't picked up my call. It increased my overthinking. I was checking my phone after every 10-15 minutes. But she didn't call me back. After 3-4 days, she called me. She said in a low voice,

Kaira : Hi. Did you called?

Vihan : Yes, I did. Where were you? You didn't even picked up my call.

Kaira : Sorry. I was busy in my work.

Vihan : Are you sure you are telling me the truth?

Kaira : Yes, I am. Bye.

Vihan : Wait......

She disconnected the call and it made my overthinking even more worse. I was not able to concentrate on my work. But I know that she will definitely come on Christmas. So, I started waiting for Christmas. But why is her behaviour changing towards me?

CHAPTER NINE

Destiny

It was Christmas Eve. I reached the location we decided and I started waiting for everyone, but I was thinking about Kaira. I texted her to reach quickly and then I called Kabir,

Vihan : Is everything going well?

Kabir : Yes, I am at Aisha's apartment.

Vihan : Okay. And listen, try to make conversation a bit romantic.

Kabir : Okay. She is coming. I'll talk to you later. Bye.

Vihan : Bye.

After this conversation, I opened up my phone's gallery and started looking at some pictures of Kaira. When I was looking at her, I heard a voice, "Looking at my eyes?"

Kaira was there. I panicked. "No No... Actually I was... Yes I was looking into your eyes.", I said. "You really like my eyes.", She said.

"No."

"Are you serious?", She said in a confused tone.

"I mean yeah I like your eyes but I also like your cute nose, your little hands, your adorable smile, your hair, your behaviour, your nature and the most important, your presence in my life."

"I am sorry Vihan."

"Oh, I was waiting for that only."

"Don't tease me Vihan. I am sorry for not picking up your calls and replying to your messages."

"Don't worry. I am glad to know that you are fine."

"Vihan I have to tell you something."

"Yes, go on."

"Do you remember the day we were listening to music together?"

"Yes, I do remember."

"And I told you that I have an important meeting the next day."

"Yeah. So?"

"So, actually...."

"Hey Kaira.", Said Aisha. Aisha and Kabir arrived. "Where is Manish?"

"Oh, he is coming. Have a seat.", I replied.

Finally Manish arrived and he gave Aisha that page.

"What is this Manish?"

"Have a look.", Manish said.

She started reading,

Hi Aisha,

I am Kabir. I have written this for you and I'll be very honest in saying this to you. I love you Aisha. The moment I broke up with you, was very tensed and I took my decision very quickly. But since that day, I can't remember a day I haven't think about you or I haven't missed you. I still remember those beautiful moments we spent together in our college time. It has been 4 years since we last spent some good time together. You still come in my dreams, the dreams that I think should never end. In this realistic world, I want you to enter the world of my imagination in which we are together and there's no one to bother us. The day when I met you after 4 years, was completely unexpected for me. I never thought that we would meet again ever. But destiny wants us to be together. So, Aisha think a hundred times before answering and look at me,

Aisha looked at Kabir,

"Will you marry me, Aisha?"

"Yes. Kabir. I love you Kabir. I love you so much.", She said and started crying happily. They both hugged each other. But I was wondering that whether Manish had written all this? I can't believe it.

I was thinking that what would have happened if it was me who proposed Kaira.

I looked at Kaira and she was clapping. But she was looking very tensed about something too. I whispered in her ear, "Is everything alright?"

"Yes.", She replied.

We all celebrated Christmas Eve together. After the celebration, when everyone left, I asked Kaira, "Would you like go on a walk?"

"No, I am okay."

I hold her hands and said, "Look at me Kaira." She wasn't looking at me. I said once more, "Look at me Kaira." And pulled her chin up towards me.

"You can tell me what's going on. I have never seen you like this before. Do you remember? You said that you chose me, so that I'll take care of you. So tell me."

She hugged me and started crying.

"Vihan. I am sorry.", She said and ran away. I followed her.

"Kaira listen... Stop Kaira please."

She stopped and came towards me and said softly, "I'll text you and please don't follow me now."

She took a taxi and left. I was standing there and wasn't able to do anything. I went home and started waiting for her message.

CHAPTER TEN

Love is a Magic

After a week of waiting for her message, I decided to call her. I called her but she didn't pick up my call. After 10-15 minutes, she called me back.

Kaira : Hi

(She was speaking quietly)

Vihan : Are you busy?

Kaira : Actually I am in my office. Is it urgent?

Vihan : No. Actually you said that you'll call me or text me... On Christmas, I hope you remember it.

Kaira : Yes, I said and I remember.... Are you free this Saturday?

Vihan : Actually I am not but I'll manage.

Kaira : Okay. So pick me up from my apartment at 6 PM on Saturday. I have to tell you something important.

Vihan : Okay ma'am. Now focus on your work or your boss will fire you.

Kaira : Okay sir. From now onwards, you are my boss.

Vihan : Really? So do you work or I'll cut your wages. (I said in a bossy tone)

Kaira : Okay boss. Bye

Vihan : Bye.

This call made me relaxed. I was very tensed about her for the last 2 weeks.

On Saturday, I reached her apartment. I bought a flower for her. She came and I gave that flower to her.

"That's so sweet.", She said.

"So, you were going to tell me something. Go on.",
I asked her.

"I will tell you. Wait. First let's go somewhere. I am
feeling hungry."

"Okay. Let's go."

We visited the café, at which we met for the first
time. 'The Hazel's Café'. We travelled a lot. We ate
many things. At last, she said, "One last place Vihan,
please. It's the last one, I promise."

"Okay. Tell me where to go."

She said softly, "Our favourite place."

"Here we go."

We reached there. She held my hand and took me
with her.

"Come sit.", She said. "Do you remember? The
promise you made me?"

"Yes, I do remember."

"Okay. Then tell me."

"Okay. I promise you that I'll never leave you until
I found someone who has better eyes than you."

"Good. I thought you might have forgotten it."

"No No. I remember."

"By the way, which type of girls do you like?"

"What?"

"Tell me Vihan."

"Umm... I haven't think about it. But I must say a
girl like you would be a great choice."

"Oh!"

"Yeah."

"And what are your thoughts on love?"

"Why are you asking these questions to me?"

"Answer me Vihan. Please."

"I think loving someone is a like magic."

"How?"

"Tell me. Why do you feel good around me?"

"I don't know. It's just a feeling which I can't express."

"Okay. For example, I love someone. I have a feeling for that girl. I want that girl to be with me. Why does this happen? And only with that girl only?... Only because I love her. It's a magic. How one person comes in your life and from nowhere, you start to love that person."

"But what if that person leaves?"

"According to me, each and every person should love someone, because it gives them a reason to smile, to live, to have a aim in their life, but on the other hand they should also have the power to not have it in their life. If a person you love, is in your life, make him or her laugh, keep them safe, treat them with care, respect them but if they leave you, don't become sad. Smile and say, 'I don't care what he or she feels about me. I am happy because I treated that person the way I loved him or her.' And move on."

"Oh! But what if that person is not able to move on."

"Tell that person to love someone again. He'll again find a reason to smile."

"Okay Okay. Enough for today."

"By the way, is there something special today?"

"No. Why?"

"Because today someone is talking about love."

"Shut up.", and she started laughing.

"Shall we go now?", She asked.

"Yes let's go."

We reached her apartment.

"Now tell me.", I said her. "You told me to wait and I waited."

"Oh! First promise me something."

"What?"

"That you'll not become angry or sad?"

"Okay. I promise."

"Actually the day we listened songs together, I told you about the meeting I had the very next day. So…"

"So… What?"

"In that meeting, it was decided that I'll be shifted to Mussoorie for 2 years, and then they'll keep shifting me from one place to another."

(This information broke my heart.)

"Oh! So when are you leaving?"

"Tomorrow."

"And you are telling me this now Seriously?"

"I am sorry Vihan."

"I wasn't expecting this from you Kaira."

"Sorry Vihan.", And she started crying softly.

"You promised on forever and now you are leaving."

"Don't worry Vihan, we'll keep meeting each other."

And suddenly I remember Kabir's and Aisha's break up story. It was also because of that long distance thing and I decided to not repeat that mistake.

"Okay. But promise me that you will call me daily and keep in touch with me. We'll meet regularly after every 6-8 months. Is that okay?"

"Okay Vihan."

"Kaira, look at me."

(She looked at me.)

"If our friendship, relationship or whatever you say, was meant to be forever then I'll try my one thousand percent to make it happen but for this I'll need you. Will you help me?"

"Yes Vihan. I will.", And she hugged me.

(I wiped her tears.)

"Now smile."

(She smiled.)

"Good."

"Okay. Then bye."

"Bye. I'll come to drop you tomorrow. Just text me the time and the place."

"Okay Vihan, and thanks for being such a great part of my life."

"You too."

"Bye"

"Bye"

CHAPTER ELEVEN

Long Distance

After dropping Kaira at her apartment, when I was going back to my home, all the flashes were going through my head. All those moments, when we were together, promises we made to each other, our favourite place, the song which she sang for me….everything. I was preparing myself for each and every circumstance, so that we could be together in future.

While I was thinking about this, a phone call came. It was an unknown number. I picked up the call,

Vihan : Hello? Who's speaking?

Unknown : Come on Vihan. You know me very well.

Vihan : I really don't know who you are. Are you going to tell me? So that I can tell whether I know you or not.

Unknown : I am Siddharth. Remember me?

Vihan : Siddharth Gupta, right?

Siddharth : Yes-Yes. From your school.

Vihan : Oh! I remember. How are you?

Siddharth : I am fine. Actually I am here in Delhi, and I am not able to find a hotel. I had your number, so I decided to ask you for some help.

Vihan : Oh!

Siddharth : So can you help me? I am stuck here.

I looked at my watch and it was 9 PM.

Vihan : Okay. Send me your location. I am coming.

Siddharth : Sure. See you.

He texted me his location. I went there and he was standing there with his luggage.

"Hey man.", I said and greeted him with a handshake.

"Hi. Thanks for helping."

"No problem."

We put his luggage inside my car.

"So, what brings you here?", I asked him.

"I am here for some official work.", He replied.

"Oh!.... By the way, how's Vanya?"

Vanya was his girlfriend in school. He was in my class and Vanya was one class junior to us.

"She is amazing. You know her."

"Yes.... I can't believe that you are still together."

"Sometimes, I also couldn't believe it. I think, it was meant to be forever and that's why our relationship is still going and we are planning to get married."

"That's really great."

"Yes.... By the way, are you still single or do you have a girlfriend... or a wife?"

"I can't say it literally. Like, I don't know what's going on."

"Why? What's going on?"

"Leave it man. I'll tell you some other day."

"Tell me Vihan."

Kaira popped up in my mind. She also used to say 'Tell me Vihan'.

"So..."

"Finally."

"Now let me speak."

"Okay. Go on."

"So there's a girl. We met recently. But in a short period of time, we made a lot of memories. I started to have feelings for her. I don't know whether she loves me or not but she used to say that she feels good around me. We became very good friends. I met her parents too. They also liked me. Almost two weeks ago I met her parents and since then things started to change. This Christmas Eve, we met and she was crying when she was leaving. It made me very tense but today I met her again. We spent very good time together but at the end of the day, she told me that she is leaving Delhi because of her job. She is going to Mussoorie, for 2 years and she'll be shifted from one place to another regularly. I don't know how to handle a long distance relationship or friendship, whatever you say. But I'll try my best. That's all I can do.", I was having tears in my eyes. I took a long breath, wiped my tears and smiled.

"That's sad."

"Yes. It is."

"Should I tell you something, to motivate you?"

"Yes. Go on."

"During our farewell party, me and Vanya decided that we'll be together always. I was going to Mumbai for my college. We agreed on our long distance relationship. After sometime, I started feeling lonely and disconnected. We used to text each other daily, video call also. But after 4-5 months, we used to meet. And that day meant everything to me that time. When we used to see each other after a long time, that feeling, that moment when she came running towards me and hugged me very tightly, was really amazing. After 4 years, when I came back, I realised, if you truly love someone, time, money, distance etc. doesn't matters. What matters is your loyalty, respect you give to each other, understanding between you, how much you care about your partner and the most important question, that you should ask yourself, 'Will you be able to love your partner for the rest of your life or not?'. Now think and decide Vihan."

I took a pause, thought about it and said,

"Thanks Siddharth."

"No problem Vihan."

"Okay. Enough for today."

"Yes. Let's change the vibe."

"So, when's you wedding?"

.

.

.

.

.

.

.

.

CHAPTER TWELVE
Gifts

Siddharth and I reached the hotel. I was about to leave but then I stopped and called him. "Hey! Siddharth.", he turned back.

"Yes?"

"Do you want to meet your sister-in-law?"

"Oh-ho! From friends to directly sister-in-law?"

"I mean future sister-in-law.", I grinned.

"Yeah sure. I am free tomorrow."

"Okay. See you tomorrow."

"Okay Vihan. Bye."

"Bye."

I reached home but I wasn't able to sleep. It was 3 AM when I decided something. I decided to give Kaira a gift, which will make her miss me. I called Kabir and Manish,

Vihan : Listen, you fools.

Kabir (In sleepy voice) : It's 3 AM. Are you mad?

Manish : Let me sleep, you motherf****r.

(Manish hung up the call)

I called him again,

Manish : What's wrong? Are you mad or what?

Vihan : Listen, it's urgent.

Kabir : So say.

Vihan : Kaira is leaving.

Manish and Kabir (Together) : What?

Vihan : Yeah. She is leaving Delhi.

Kabir : When?

Vihan : Tomorrow.

Manish : So call me tomorrow. Bye.

Vihan : Wait-wait, Manish.

Manish : Hmm.

Vihan : I was thinking that I should gift her something.

Kabir : So, what will you gift her?

Manish : Cond*ms?

Kabir : Shut up.

Manish : Leave the gift. Just ask her for farewell s*x. I'll book the hotel.

Vihan : Are you drunk?

Kabir : Leave him. Let me call Aisha. She'll help.

Vihan : What if she's sleeping?

Kabir : Relax buddy.

He called Aisha.

Aisha : What happened Kabir? Are you still missing me?

Kabir : You are on a conference call with Vihan and Manish.

Aisha : Oh! Sorry sorry.

Manish : Actually, I was missing you.

Aisha : Are you drunk?

Kabir : Leave him and listen to me.

Aisha : Yes?

Kabir : Kaira is leaving Delhi tomorrow.

Aisha : Yeah. I know.

Vihan : What? So, why didn't you tell me Aisha?

Aisha : She told me not to tell anyone. So I didn't. I am sorry.

Kabir : It's Okay Aisha. So Vihan has decided to give a gift to her. Can you suggest something?

Aisha : I don't know much about her. I mean what she likes and what she don't.

Vihan : Anything girls like?

Aisha : Umm... Girls like...

Manish : A handsome boy like me.

Kabir : This bastard won't stop.

Aisha : You can gift her something permanent.

Vihan : Like?

Kabir : A dress? A locket? A ring?

Manish : Give me as a gift to her.

Vihan : Meet me tomorrow Manish. I'll punch you very tightly in your face.

Aisha : Gift her a photo frame. In which we all are there.

Vihan : It's a good idea. I'll think.

Manish : Does she know that you like her?

Vihan : No. Not till now.

Aisha : You like her?

Vihan : Yes Aisha. I do. I don't only like her, I love her.

Aisha : Is there a difference?

Vihan : Yes?

Aisha : What?

Vihan : I'll tell you some other day.

Manish : Kabir bro. Handle him otherwise it'll be him who will marry Aisha, not you.

Kabir : Shut up Manish, please.

Vihan : Okay. So I'll text you time and location tomorrow, when I'll get to know. Bye.

Kabir : Bye.

Aisha : Bye Vihan.

Manish (In a funny and sleepy tone) : Bye Aisha. I love you Aisha. Muaaahhh. Bye bye.

Kabir : You.....

I hung up the call. I was planning everything in my mind about what will happen tomorrow but I was tensed too. Next day, when I woke up, I saw a message. It was Kaira's message. She sent me the time and location. I forwarded it to Kabir, Aisha, Manish and Siddharth. I got ready and left for Kaira's gift. I reached the shop and asked the shopkeeper to make a photo frame. I gave him the photograph and he said, "You'll get it till evening."

"What? Can't you give it to me till afternoon?"

"I'll try."

"I'll pay extra. Please."

"Listen. We have about 20-30 incomplete orders."

"It's urgent to me. Please, I request you."

"Sorry, but I'll try my best."

It made me a bit angry and I said in a bit louder voice, "Try to understand. She's leaving." I took a pause, made myself calm and said, "I am sorry."

He made a confused face for a second and then he said, "How much do you love her?"

I was shocked but I answered, "A lot. Try to understand. Please."

He showed me a photograph of a girl and said, "Look at her. I also loved her. She left and never came back."

"I am sorry."

"But... I don't want ruin your story. So I'll make it."

I joined my hands and said, "Thank you. Thank you."

"But promise me, you'll complete your story."

"I'll try my best."

"Okay. It'll be done till afternoon."

"Thanks. I'll come."

CHAPTER THIRTEEN

DDLJ

I came out of the shop and called Kaira.

Vihan : Hi. Where are you?

Kaira : I am at my home. Why?

Vihan : Nothing. I was thinking that... Can I come?

Kaira : Why? If I may ask, my Boss.

Vihan : Just to see you.

Kaira : But....

Vihan : No ifs and buts. I am coming.

Kaira : Okay. I am waiting.

Vihan : Wear something red.

Kaira : But...

Vihan : Pleeeaaase.

Kaira : Okay. You fool.

I hung up the call. I drove my car straight to Kaira's apartment. I rang the door bell and when she opened the gate, I got scared.

"Whoooooo.", I said.

"It's me, Kaira.", She replied.

"What happened to your face?"

"It's a face mask, you idiot."

"Oh! You scared me."

She laughed and said, "You are such a character. Come in."

I entered.

"Wait. I am coming in 10 minutes."

"Okay... By the way, where are you going."

"I am going to take a bath."

"Shall I come inside?"

She laughed, "Shut up... 10 minutes only."

I started roaming here and there. She was all packed to leave. Suddenly, I saw a diary on her table. I picked up that diary and started reading it.

"Page no. 241 –

Dear diary,

Today I am very happy. I am happily crying. It was my interview-day today. I was really nervous but still I answered each and every question with confidence. When I came out, I was very tensed. After some time, interviewer came and said, 'You are selected. You have to go to Delhi and there you will be informed what to do next.'. I came home and told my parents that I am selected and they were very happy. I hugged my father and he said, 'Well done. I am proud of you, my daughter.'. Then we went out to celebrate and enjoyed a lot. I hope you are excited too after listening to this and just a reminder, I am going to Delhi, next week. Now I am going to sleep. So good night."

It just smiled and started turning pages to my birthday. I started reading,

"Page no. 249 –

Dear diary,

I want to tell you something. Today, in the morning, I was feeling very lonely and I was missing my Mom-Dad too and I had to go to my office also. It was my first day. I took a metro. I was texting my mom that I am really missing her. Suddenly, I looked up and I saw a boy staring at me. I looked in his eyes and passed a smile. It was very strange. But... In the evening, when I was returning back, I was in a metro and I saw that same boy entering. Seat beside me was empty, but still he was standing right in front of me.

So, I asked him to sit. He was looking very shy, so, I started the conversation. I said, 'I know you.'.

'So tell me something about myself.', he looked into my eyes and said.

Also, in the morning, he was looking into my eyes. So I took a guess and said, 'You like my eyes, right?', and this way, we started talking. He talked to me very politely and I came to know that it was his birthday today. I really enjoyed talking to him and he genuinely seemed like a nice person to me. So, I took his number and I came home. I really don't know why, but I think, in the near future, if everything went well, then I am going to start loving him. Okay, enough for today. Good night."

After reading that page, I was not having tears in my eyes. I was having tears in my heart. I heard the door sound from behind, so, I closed the diary and kept it back. I turned and I saw Kaira in a red dress. She asked me, "How am I looking?". I went straight to her and hugged her. She hugged me back and said, "What happened Vihan?"

"Just keep holding me tightly.", and a tear falled from my eye. I wiped my tear.

"Okay Vihan. Let me get ready."

I stepped back and said, "Okay."

She was going towards her room. I said, "Kaira."

"Yes Vihan?"

"You're looking like a princess."

"But I don't have a prince Vihan."

In my mind, I said, "You have. Just don't go please."

In reality, I said, "One day you'll definitely get a prince, who'll be better than me."

"I don't wish the same."

She got ready.

"Let's go.", I said and I was about to leave her room. She called me and said, "Will you let me go today in a normal way or in a filmy way? Like DDLJ."

"I don't want you to go but I also don't want to you to choose me over your career. So I don't know how I'll react."

"Just react normally, you idiot."

"I'll try. Now shall we go?", I smiled and said.

"Yeah. Let's gooooo."

Such a crazy girl she is.

CHAPTER FOURTEEN
Farewell

Me and Kaira got in my car and left her apartment. We reached the station 30 minutes early, at 3 PM. As we reached, I introduced Kaira to Siddharth, and Siddharth to all of them.

"Hey everyone, meet Siddharth. He's my school friend. And Siddharth, meet Kaira, Aisha, Kabir and Manish.", I introduced them.

"Kaira, I am going to miss you.", Aisha said and hugged her.

Kabir said, "I hope that we'll meet again in future. All the best for your career." And hugged her.

Siddharth said, "I am not going to miss you but I'll definitely wish that you'll have a great success in future."

Manish said, "Why are going? Just stay with us."

"I too want to stay but.. I have to go.", Kaira said.

"Okay. But when you reach there, don't forget to call us regularly.", Manish said and hugged her.

"Guys. I am really going to miss you all.", Kaira said.

"We too. But not more than Vihan.", Manish said. Such a bad secret keeper.

She blushed and I smiled.

After all this, Aisha looked at me in a strange way and said, "Can I talk to Vihan for 2 minutes?"

"Kabir, I told you that in the near future he'll marry her, not you. Kaira is leaving, so, Vihan is looking for someone else.", Manish said.

Kaira looked at me and blushed again.

"Shut up Manish.", Aisha said, grabbed my hand and took me away from them.

"Where's the photo frame Vihan?"

"Holy-Shit. I forgot about it."

"Go and get it fast. We have only 30 minutes left."

I ran towards my car. I drove my car very fast, directly to that shop. I reached there at 3.20 PM.

"Uncle, where's the photo frame?"

"Wait."

"Fast, uncle."

He gave me the photo frame and when I was leaving in a hurry, he said, "Listen."

I stopped.

"I want your love story to be completed, happily.... All the best.", He said.

I turned back and said, "Thank you Uncle. I'll try as much as I can to complete my story."

I again drove my car very fast to the station. I reached there at 3.35 PM. I saw she was on the train and the train started to move. I ran, and ran ,and ran. Finally, I reached her train cabin and gave her the photo frame.

"Kaira...", I was breathing heavily and she was looking into my eyes. "It's a gift from my side...", She had tears in her eyes. "Don't cry. I am here with you.", I said.

"I know, you idiot."

Now, we both had tears in our eyes.

"I'll miss you."

"Not more than me. I bet."

And her train left the station.

I wiped my tears and came back to my friends. I was looking very sad. So, Kabir, Aisha and Manish hugged me. I looked at Siddharth standing there. I asked him to join. He also came and hugged me.

"Don't worry Vihan. We are here with you.", Aisha said.

"Yes Vihan. If you ever feel lonely, or need s*x, Aisha is here.", Manish said and ran.

"Today you'll die Manish.", Kabir said and ran to catch him. We all laughed.

"Okay Vihan. I have to go now.", Siddharth said.

I replied, "Okay and thanks for coming."

"No problem Vihan. Just remember, anytime you need me, just call me."

"Okay. Bye."

"Bye."

"Bye", Aisha said.

Siddharth left.

"Let's go.", Aisha said. I again remember Kaira. She also used to say that, "Let's go.". I replied, "Okay."

As soon as I was leaving, I got a text message. It was Kaira's message,

Kaira : (Her photograph with that photo frame.)

Her phone call arrived,

Kaira : Vihan, thank you so so so so so... much for this gift. It's the best gift I ever received in my entire life.

Vihan : You're welcome Kaira.

Kaira : By the way, I already started missing you.

Vihan (sarcastically): Then come back.

Kaira : Shut up Vihan. You're such a character.

A flashback came. She said it when we met for the first time in metro.

Vihan : I think, it's only because of the time I spent with you. I also became a cartoon like you.

Kaira : I am not a cartoon, okay? You are a cartoon.
Vihan : Okay. My little cartoon.
Kaira : Stop teasing me.
Vihan : No... Never...
Kaira : Okay. Then, bye I guess.
Vihan : No, no. I was just kidding.
Kaira : I mean really, bye.
Vihan : Text me when you reach there.
Kaira : Okay Boss.
Vihan : Bye.

CHAPTER FIFTEEN

Happy Birthday

After Kaira left, I used to miss her a lot. We used to talk to each other through video calls and mostly through messages because, the network there, in Mussoorie, was very slow. My entire day went into my work but during the night... I can't express. After working for an entire day, I do not used to take some rest, I do not used to have my dinner. The first thing I used to do is to message Kaira, and then we used to talk. Everything was going well. But sometimes Kaira starts to cry during video call because she really misses me too. I used to console her, I do a lot of crazy shit to make her laugh, we send our photos to each other, make romantic plans and many such things. In between, we celebrated her birthday. Unfortunately we couldn't get time to meet each other. So we celebrated it online through a video call.

10 months later, we were on a video call,

Vihan : Do you know which date is tomorrow?

Kaira : Yes. It's 19th November. But why?

Vihan : Are you sure that you are not forgetting something?

Kaira : Don't create suspense please. Tell me.

Vihan : Come on Kaira. You are literally the dumbest girl in this entire universe.

Kaira (Crying in a funny way) : Tell me Vihan.

Vihan : Okay. Tomorrow is my birthday.

Kaira : Holy sh*t. How can I forget about it?

Vihan : Yeah.

Kaira : I am sorry Vihan.

Vihan : I won't say it's okay. You made me angry. Now convince me that you are actually sorry.

Kaira : Okay. So, What should I do to convince you, sir?

Vihan : I don't know, you made me angry.

Kaira : Okay. I'll take a leave tomorrow to come and meet you. Is that okay?

Vihan : What? You are kidding me? I am not dumb.

Kaira : Vihan relax. I'll come.

Vihan : Are you sure that you will come?

Kaira : I am not sure completely but 90 percent of the chances are, that I'll come.

Vihan : You made my entire day amazing. Thank you.

Kaira : Do you remember that one year ago, I told you that we'll celebrate your birthday some other day.

Vihan : Yes, I do remember.

.

.

.

.

.

And our conversation continued.

Kaira hung up the call and I instantly called Kaira and Manish.

Vihan : Hello listen.

Kabir : Speak fast, I am busy.

Manish : He's having s*x. Hello Aisha? Are you there?

Vihan : Listen Manish. It's serious.

Manish : Okay.

Vihan : Kaira is coming tomorrow.

Aisha (From Kabir's phone) : What?

Manish : So there you are. Vihan I already told you.

Kabir : Manish, we were just going to bed. Can't you become serious in your life?

Manish : No. I can't live a life, where fun and entertainment is not there.

Kabir : Okay. Then don't interrupt and Fu*k off. You carry on Vihan.

Vihan : I am meeting her after a long time. So what should I do?

Manish : Try to make it romantic.

Vihan : But how?

Kabir : Listen. Leave it on us, we'll manage. Just go and sleep.

Vihan : You'll mess things up.

Kabir : Vihan. Trust me. I promise I'll handle it. Just meet me at the given location tomorrow along with Kaira.

Vihan : Okay. Now it's on you.

Aisha (Again from Kabir's phone) : And don't forget to pick her from the station.

Kabir : Take some flowers also.

Vihan : Okay goodnight.

Manish : Now jerk off and sleep.

Vihan : Fu*k off you bastard.

Next day, I reached the airport to receive Kaira. I took a white flower with me. As she arrived, I was really happy. I went running towards her, she also came running towards me, I gave that white flower to her. We hugged each other very tightly and I closed my eyes because I was feeling her presence after 10 months.

"Happy Birthday Vihan."

"Thank you Kaira."

It made me a bit emotional and at that time, I realised that Siddharth was right. Meeting a person you love, after a very long time makes you really happy. When we were hugging each other, someone called Kaira.

"Who's he Kaira?"

It was a man's voice. I looked at him and he was standing beside me and Kaira. He was a bit taller than me and he had a good physique too.

"He's my best friend, Vinay.", She replied.

He said, "Oh! Hi man." And greeted me with a handshake.

"By the way, I just heard Kaira wishing you a Happy Birthday. So happy birthday from my side too brother."

"Thanks Vinay."

"Sorry but what's your name?"

"My name is Vihan."

"Nice to meet you Vihan. Shall we go now?"

"Yeah sure."

Who's this guy? How do he know Kaira? And the main question, what the fu*k is he doing here?

CHAPTER SIXTEEN

Possessiveness

We were in my car. Vinay was sitting on the back seat, Kaira was sitting beside me and I was driving the car.

"So, what's the plan, birthday boy.", Kaira said.

"Nothing much. Firstly, we will go to my house, so that you can have some rest and then in the afternoon, we all will celebrate.", I replied.

"Will you come Vinay?", Kaira asked.

Why the fu*k is she inviting him?

"Only if Vihan wants me to come.", He said.

"Yeah yeah. You can come.", I said.

(Motherfu**er)

"Great.", Said Kaira.

"Vinay.", I said.

"Yes?"

"How do you know Kaira?"

"Actually he is my boss's son.", Kaira interrupted. "I asked my boss for a leave but he said that he'll grant me a leave only for one day because I have a lot of work to do there. And he also asked me to take Vinay with me because Vinay likes travelling. And he had never come to Delhi before."

"Oh! So you'll leave tonight?", I asked.

"Yes. I have to.", She replied.

We arrived at my house.

"Where's the washroom?", Vinay asked.

I pointed towards the gate and he went inside.

"Where are Manish, Kabir and Aisha?", Kaira asked.

"They'll meet us in the evening. Do you need some rest?"

"No I just want some water."

"Just wait."

I poured some water for her.

"Thank you."

"Can I ask you a question?", I asked.

"Yes. Go on."

I was about to ask her that does she thinks that vinay loves her or not. But I didn't ask.

"Leave it."

"Vihan, you can ask me anything."

"Nothing. I was just thinking something."

"Vihan. Are you sure?"

"Yeah."

I was sitting far from her. So, I headed towards her and sat beside her. I looked into her eyes. She was also looking directly into my eyes.

"Oh my god! I really missed those beautiful eyes.", I said.

We closed our eyes and I held her hand in my hand. We came more closer to each other. We were in our romantic zone. We were heading towards our first kiss. Our lips were about to touch.

(Door opening sound)

Vinay came out of the washroom. As soon as we heard that sound, we started pretending like nothing is happening.

"Do you need some rest Vinay?", Kaira asked him.

"No. I am okay."

"Are you hungry?", I asked Kaira.

"Yes. I am."

"Wait. Let me cook for you.", Vinay said.

"You are kidding me.", Kaira said.

He laughed a bit and said, "What happened?"

"You can cook?"

"Yes, I can.", Vinay replied.

"I don't believe it."

"Come. I'll show you. Where's the kitchen Vihan?"

"There.", I replied.

(Such a bastard)

We all entered the kitchen.

"So, what would you like to eat ma'am.", Vinay asked.

"Umm.."

"She loves pasta.", I replied.

"Red or white?", Vinay said.

I said, "White."

"Do you still remember?", Kaira looked at me, smiled and asked.

"Ofcourse, I do remember Kaira.", I looked into her eyes and said.

She hugged me. I looked at Vinay and he was looking at us. He smiled and asked me for the ingredients.

He started cooking the pasta. Kaira was helping her and I was looking at her. But sometimes, they both used to come very close to each other. I hate that. And yes, I am possessive about but I just don't react. And it's not only my fault, if anyone loves someone or something, then they'll get possessive about that thing. Now some people react and complain, and some don't.

After 20-25 minutes, we were on our dining table. Vinay served pasta to us. Kaira took the first bite and got her tongue burned. I immediately brought some water for her.

"Relax..."

I was about to complete but Vinay took that glass of water from me and gave her.

"Thanks Vinay. Actually it was hot and you know how impatient I am.", Kaira said.

"Don't worry. It's okay."

Then he took some pasta in the fork, cooled it down and said, "Now, open your mouth."

"It's okay Vinay. I'll eat it."

"Kaira. Open your mouth please."

"Okay."

She opened her mouth and looked at me. She gave me a "don't worry-look" from her eyes.

"It's delicious Vinay. You cook really amazing.", Kaira appreciated.

(In my mind - "Yes Yes. He'll definitely came to our wedding and cook. MotherFu**er. Bastard. A**hole. D**k-head.")

"Vihan... Vihan... Vihaaan.", Kaira repeated my name three times.

"Yes?"

"Where were you lost?"

"No-where."

"Do you like the pasta?"

"Wait. I haven't eaten it yet."

I ate the pasta. That was really amazing. Like the most delicious and unique pasta I ever ate in my entire life. But I don't like this guy at all.

"How's it?", Vinay asked.

"It's good but it lacks some salt and oregano."

"Sorry. I tried my best.", He smiled and said. "But Kaira liked it. That's enough."

Kaira blushed and said, "Don't try to flirt with me."

I really hate this guy. Aaaaaahhhhhh.

CHAPTER SEVENTEEN

The Wine

After eating the pasta, I called Kabir.

Vihan (in low voice) : What's going on? You told me that you'll manage everything.

Kabir : Yes yes. I have managed. Just meet me at the given location.

Vihan : Okay.

I headed up straight to Kaira and said, "Come. I have a surprise for you."

"What about Vinay?"

Vinay was sitting just next to us.

"No problem Vihan. It's her surprise.", Vinay interrupted.

"Are you sure?", Kaira asked.

"Yeah. I am."

I held Kaira's hand in my hand. We sat in my car and headed directly to the given location. In between we talked a lot about our past memories. While we were talking, I got a notification on my phone.

Kabir : When you reach there, don't forget to cover Kaira's eyes.

I read the message and kept my phone aside. As soon as we reached there, I asked Kaira, "Do you mind if I close your eyes?"

"No, I won't."

I covered her eyes with a cloth. I directed him to the given location. It was a dark room. Only a dim light was glowing which was kept on the table. I was only able to see a table and that lamp on it.

"What's going on?", Kaira asked.

"Just wait."

I headed towards the table and there were two chairs there. I made her sit on one of those chairs, and then I also sat facing her. I asked Kaira to open her eyes. At first she seemed a bit afraid, because of darkness but when she saw that lamp, she became relaxed. I again got a message from Kabir.

Kabir : We can see you.

Kabir : There's a wine bottle beneath your table. Take it out and ask her for a drink.

I did the same.

"Wine?"

"Of course."

I started pouring the wine.

"By the way, I have never drink wine before."

"Me too. Let's try it together."

I poured some wine.

"One... Two... Three...", We said together.

We had a sip.

"Ewww. It taste's so bad.", She said.

"Yeah. Waste of money."

Again I got a notification,

Kabir : You bastard. I paid 1000 rupees for that bottle.

"Are you busy?", Kaira asked.

"No, there's some idiot messaging me."

Kabir : You motherf***er.

Kabir : Now ask her whether she wants a surprise or not? And then snap your fingers.

"So, ready for another surprise.", I asked.

"Yes. I love surprises."

I snapped my fingers. Room got enlightened and I saw Kabir, Manish and Aisha entering. They all greeted me a very happy birthday and Kaira was shocked after seeing this. Kaira hugged Manish, Kabir and Aisha and said, "I really missed you guys."

"We missed you too Kaira.", Aisha said.

"I have a gift for you Vihan.", Manish said.

"Come on. We are not kids now.", I said.

"But we are friends, right?", Manish said.

He gave me a box. I opened it and there was a lot of cotton inside it. I took that cotton outside and there was a c**dom inside it.

"What's this Manish?", I asked angrily.

"I thought you are going to have reunion s*x? So... That's why..."

"F**k off Manish."

Then we all laughed. We celebrated my birthday. It was really a good day for me. In between, Vinay was calling Kaira after every half an hour which I didn't like at all.

Me and Kaira reached home and we saw Vinay sleeping. I took Kaira to my balcony. I brought her closer to me and we were about to kiss but she got uncomfortable and said, "Wait. Vinay will woke up."

"No, he'll not.", I whispered.

"Please try to understand Vihan."

Now all the levels were crossed. It made me angry and I said in a bit louder voice, "What's wrong with you Kaira?"

"What?"

"Really? Don't think I am a fool. I know you love Vinay. In afternoon, you ate pasta from his hands and you didn't even stopped him doing that in front of me. All the time you were in kitchen with him. He was consistently trying to come closer to you but you never did anything, and now, Vinay will see.. Vinay will see.. what's wrong with you?"

"Vihan, relax. Vinay will woke up."

"Again Vinay. Just shut up and f**k off."

I left that place. When I was leaving, I never turned back and just walked out.

After 10-20 minutes, I came back. Kaira was crying and Vinay was consoling her. She saw me and said, "Let's go Vinay."

She started packing her bag. Vinay came towards me and said, "You shouldn't have done that."

I pushed him a bit and ran towards Kaira. I said, "Kaira.. Kaira.. Kaira listen, I didn't mean to do that. I am sorry."

She didn't said a word.

"Kaira. Atleast look at me when I am talking to you."

"Are you ready Vinay?", She looked towards Vinay and said.

"Yeah."

"Kaira.", I said.

"What Kaira-Kaira-Kaira? I didn't expect this from you Vihan."

"I am sorry Kaira.", I said and grabbed her hand.

"Let me go."

"No. Not again."

"Please.", She was crying.

I released her hand and let her go. She left and a tear fell from my eye.

CHAPTER EIGHTEEN
The End

I was sitting on the edge of my bed. The echoes of the heated argument with Kaira were still resonating in my mind. I tried to call Kaira but she didn't pick it up. Suddenly a phone call came from an unknown number. I didn't receive that call. That person called again. I picked it.

Unknown : Hello.

Vihan : Yes. Who are you?

Unknown : You are Vihan, right?

Vihan : Yes, how do you know me? Who are you?

Unknown : Reach the city hospital as soon as possible. Your friends had an accident.

Vihan : What?

Unknown : My phone doesn't have enough battery. Come fast.

This made me tensed. I instantly picked up my car and reached the hospital. As soon as I reached there, I called that person.

Vihan : Where are you?

Unknown : Right in front of the ICU.

I reached there. I saw that person. He told me, "Listen Vihan. A truck hit her her car. She was badly wounded and your other friend is in the patient ward. I immediately took her phone but her phone was not working properly. So I checked her purse and from her diary I got your number."

"Okay Uncle. Thank you."

I rushed towards the patient ward. Vinay was there. He had multiple fractures. I went there.

"Hey man.", I said slowly.

"Hi."

Silence entered our conversation. I was feeling very sad. I realised how stupid I was. Vinay broke the silence.

"Vihan."

"Yes?"

"Do you think that I love her?"

"No no."

"Don't lie. I listened to your conversation, with Kaira."

"Ok."

"Listen Vihan. I don't love her. I was just trying to flirt with her but I really didn't knew that you guys love each other."

"And now, you know, right?"

"Yeah. Kaira told me."

"What?"

"We were in the taxi, heading towards the airport. She was crying. I asked her that whether she loves you or not. She said that she loves you more than you think. She showed me your photographs in her mobile phone. She also told me about how you guys met each other and came close. She really loves you a lot, Vihan."

This made me emotional. I started crying.

"Thanks Vinay. Get well soon."

I again headed towards the ICU. I saw Kaira from the window. She was badly wounded. Her head, her hands, her legs, everything was badly injury. I turned back. I called Kabir, Aisha, Manish and her parents. They reached the hospital. I told them about the accident. They were shocked too. In between, I asked a doctor, "Sir, how's she?"

"She's is not fine at all. Just pray for her."

I didn't slept that night. Next day, when there was no energy left inside me, I ate something and slept there only. When I woke up, doctors were coming and going from ICU. I again asked, "How's she?"

Doctor replied, "Her situation is critical."

Kabir came towards me and said, "Go home, take some rest. We are here."

"No Kabir."

"Vihan. Look at me."

I looked at him with tears in my eyes. He wiped my tears and said, "Go."

"Promise me you'll keep me updated."

"Promise."

I went home, took a shower and went to a temple. I prayed there for Kaira's recovery.

I said to God, "I don't know if she'll survive or not, but please God, it's my request, let her live. I really love her. She means everything to me."

I also went to the shop from where I had got the photo frame made for her. I reached there and told the uncle, "Uncle. I told you that I'll complete my story but today she's not well. I don't know if she'll survive or not. So, I apologise."

"Have some faith son. In God, in love. She'll survive."

"I hope so."

Each and every day, I used to visit Kaira. She was so badly injured that she couldn't even speak. In visiting hours, I used to sit beside her and tell her about those beautiful memories we made.

10 days later, I came to hospital and doctor called me in his cabin.

"What happened, doctor?"

"She's fine and we are planning to discharge her within a week if reports are okay."

This news made me happy.

"Thank you doctor."

"By the way, she is able to speak now. You can go and talk to her."

"Okay sir."

As I was leaving his cabin he called, "Vihan."

"Yes sir."

"Do you know what her first words were, when she started speaking?"

"What?"

"She asked about you. She said, 'Where is Vihan?' Now go and meet her with a smile on your face."

I rushed towards ICU. She was there.

"Hi Kaira."

"Hello Vihan."

"I love you Kaira."

"I love you too Vihan."

"Please get well soon. I am missing you so much."

"Me too.... Vihan, I am sorry."

"Shhh. No need to say that. Just get well soon."

Nurse entered and said, "Times up sir."

I said to Kaira, "Okay. Now I am leaving. I'll wait for you."

"Vihan. One last thing."

"Yes."

"Promise me that you'll take me to our favourite place when I'll be discharged."

"Okay. I promise."

I kissed on her forehead and left.

After a week, she was finally discharged and as promised, I took her to our favourite place. We went there, sat on that bench. It was 6 p.m. The sunset was looking very beautiful.

"When I met you for the first time, I thought you must have been very irritating and so annoying, but as our meetings increased and I got to know you, I realized how stupid I was when I thought about you like that. The best thing I ever experienced in my life is your presence.", I said to her and then I came closer to her to kiss her. I had a Déjà vu, like this has happened before.

She came closer to me. Her lips met mine and after a long kiss I said, "You're 'Perfect for Me'."